TAKING WHAT'S HERS

LOVE & DECEIT BOOK 1

MIA BLACK

D1523212

PROLOGUE

I hid behind the door, hoping that he couldn't hear my heavy breathing. I heard him scream for me.

"Kiyana! Quit with the bullshit. I'm going to eventually find you."

I heard him walking across the room, the scraping of his shoes against the hardwood floors coming closer and closer to my hiding place. I peeped through the slats in the door as he approached and slammed his hands against the door. I thought he was going to break the door down. I stepped back into the closet and silently prayed that Zerek or even his wife would come back. I saw his hands reach for the door-knob and I prepared myself to be snatched up and pulled out of the closet. I looked for a weapon to protect myself, but the only thing I saw was Candace's fur coats and Zerek's leather trenches. I was fucked.

Then all of a sudden, there was silence. I heard his feet move away from the closet and go up the wooden staircase. I cautiously crawled out of the closet and hid behind the plush white leather couch. I looked around and didn't see any sight of the man. He was still upstairs looking for me. I knew then that I had to make my move. It was now or never. Taking one more glance around me, I stood up and made a break for it. I was a star sprinter for my high school. I won numerous awards, and my body still had the definition. I ran on my toes, using all of my power to make a beeline for the front door, which was a good fifty feet away from the main living room. The expensive artwork, the original Basquiats and Warhols, became a blur as I ran for the double French doors that led to my freedom.

Just as I was about to open the door, I felt a hand grip my hair and yank me back with such intensity that I thought my neck was going to break. I fell down on the hardwood floor. As I writhed in pain, I looked up at the barrel of a shotgun. My heart froze. I never thought he would hurt me. I had been nothing but good to him, but I had to go. I had no choice, he was bad for me. But here I was staring at the barrel of a gun, with his finger on the trigger.

There was no escaping this. I tried to scream, I tried to talk some sense into him, but I couldn't find the words. There was nowhere I could run or hide. My life was truly over. I was dead and none of my family knew where I was.

In my mind, I said a quick prayer to God to forgive me for everything. With a single tear streaming down my face, I closed my eyes and waited for him to pull the trigger.

CHAPTER 1

Miami is known for many things: beautiful women, mansions, expensive cars and a party scene that rivals Ibiza. Even though it's expensive as hell, and competition is everywhere, I don't see myself living anywhere else but here. I was Miami-born and raised and had the hazel eyes, bronze skin and bikini-ready body to prove it. I was Afro-Cubana and was always quick to represent.

We Miami women are a different breed. We always stay fly because you just never know who you might meet while sunning in SoBe or shopping at Lincoln Square. With so many ballers in the area, a five-minute conversation could turn into a yacht ride to the Florida Keys or courtside seats to a Miami Heat game.

I'll admit in my past, I did enjoy quite a few of those nights, but unlike the other gorgeous chicks that cat-walked on the Miami streets, I chose to go the schoolgirl route. I was the star track and field runner at my high school, which I parlayed into a full ride scholarship to run for the Gators. I then graduated from FSU with my bachelor's in nursing, finishing summa cum laude. Beauty was easy to come by, but brains, that's another thing. When you have that combination plus you had that good good, you were truly a bad bitch, and I wore the title proudly.

I had been pursued by many men, hell I still do, but no one caught my heart the way Ty did. Even though that nigga and me had our up and downs, every time I got mad at him, I thought about the first time we met and how he swept me off my feet. My girls and I had been sunning ourselves in South Beach. We wanted to enjoy the sun before we went to Mercedes Benz Fashion Week. I was looking right in my white Fendi bikini with Fendi aviators. All of a sudden, a dark shadow appeared over me. I lowered my shades and was looking at the finest man that I ever laid eyes on. He had cinnamon brown skin and gray eyes with sandy hair. His body was chiseled to the Gods and I could tell that he was packing. My mouth dropped open for a second but I quickly composed myself.

"You're blocking my sun," I said as I laid back down on my beach pillow. He continued to stand there.

"It's the only way to get your attention," he replied.

I turned to my girl, Lauren, who was laughing silently and turned her back to me. I turned back to him and sat up, then lowered my glasses from my eyes and gave him another onceover. "So now you have my attention. Make it quick."

He reached down and offered his hand. I took it and he helped me up. Taking my hand, he twirled me around. He then stepped back and bit his lower lip, his eyes filled with appreciation. "Yes, it's you."

"Who am I?" I asked.

"My new wife."

My girls and I laughed. "Oh here you go. I thought you had something real to say." I went to sit back down, but he reached out and grabbed my arm.

"That is something real to say. When I see something I want, I go for it. You obviously don't know who you talking to. You'll see by the end of the night."

"You're not the first man to say some shit like that to me. I know how to—"

He interrupted. "But I will be the last, and you ain't never had a man like me. Like I said, you'll know by the end of the night, and you'll be mine. But until then, learn up about me." He smiled and walked off.

"Typical Miami nigga! He need to learn up about you." Lauren said as I sat down next to her.

"It's cute though, acting like we don't know. He was fine, though," I said.

"Penny a dozen," she replied.

I nodded in response, before I closed my eyes and continued to bask in the Miami sun.

I got home to my apartment around 3:30. I lived in one of the most fashionable apartment complexes in the city. It overlooked downtown Miami with a fresh ass view of the Atlantic Ocean. I stayed a little bit longer at the beach than I intended to so I had to rush to get ready for the fashion shows. My girl, Anais, was debuting her new swimsuit fashion line at Fashion Swim week. We had front row seats so we all had to look fly.

After a long shower and putting on my Nars Monoi glow, I picked out a crisp white silk romper that hugged me in all the right spots. Gold bangles, a gold Christian Dior belt and the gold Blanca gladiator sandals set my shit off just right. I put argan oil in my hair for shine and accented my lips and cheeks with Nars Orgasm lip-gloss and illuminator. I put my compact, LV key purse and gloss in my gold YSL clutch.

I gave myself a onceover. Damn, I looked good. Then I reached for my phone and texted Lauren to let her know that I would meet her at her house. I picked up my keys and opened the door to leave the house. As I walked out of my complex I noticed that parked in front of my apartment was a stretch white limo. The driver was standing outside holding a sign with my name on it. I smiled. My girls always knew how to make an entrance. I walked up to the car, and the driver opened the door for me.

"Miss Torres?" the driver asked.

"Yes."

"Right this way." He ushered me into the limo. I expected to see my girls in the car but there was no one to be found. On the seat was a bucket of ice with champagne and a glass with a note next to it. I was about to jump out of the car but the driver had already shut the door, got in the front seat and drove off. I reached over and picked up the note.

You honestly will have no choice but to be mine by the end of the night. Go get your girls, this one is on me. Like I said before, munequita, learn up about me.

Ty.

I sat back in awe. How the fuck did he find out about me? I didn't even know the nigga's name. Didn't even give him mine, either, but he knew where I was, and my ass was stupid and got in the car anyway. I'll admit luxury and money sometimes blinded me. It was something that I definitely had to work on.

We started driving. I tried to look out the windows to see where we were going, but the tint was so dark I couldn't make out any of the street signs or landmarks. After what was about ten minutes, we slowed down and pulled up to a building. The door opened and a few seconds later, my girl Lauren got into the car.

"Girl, I didn't know Anais was gonna do it big like this," Lauren said as she sat across from me.

"L, I don't know if Anais was the one who brought us the car."

Lauren raised her eyebrow as she looked at me with concern. "Then who did it?"

I simply shrugged as the driver pulled off. We rode in silence. Lauren opened up her compact and played with her sand-colored curls, while I stared straight ahead and held the note tightly in my hands. After about another twenty minutes, we stopped in front of another apartment building. A few minutes later, the door opened and my other friend, Arianna, got into the car. She smiled as she sat down and immediately reached for the champagne that was in the ice bucket.

"Pre-gaming," she said as she opened up the bottle and poured herself a glass. After she took a sip of the champagne, she looked at us and smiled. "Anais knows how to do it big. My girl is going places."

Lauren and I looked at each other and smiled at Arianna.

"I wouldn't expect anything less from her," I replied.

We continued to ride in silence for the rest of the ride. When the limo finally stopped and the door was opened to the entrance of Collins Park. As we stepped out of the car, we looked around at the white tents that dotted the landscape. We were amongst models, millionaires and moguls. We definitely blended in. Lauren looked amazing in a cobalt blue halter jumpsuit with silver heels, and Arianna stunned in a rose-colored Herve Leger body-con dress with matching Pigalle Louboutin pumps. I thanked the driver and we walked down the main entrance toward the check-in booths. We found Anais's location and made our way to her tent.

Once we got there, we were escorted to the very front, where all the stars sat. We tried our best not to embarrass ourselves by staring at them as we made our way to our seats. I beamed with pride as I looked at everything Anais had accomplished in the last two years. When she was fresh out of Parsons Design School, she already selling her crocheted bikinis on Etsy. A year later, she then opened up her own store, and by this point she was debuting next year's collection at Miami Fashion week. Bad bitches roll in packs and mine were no exception.

My girls, Lauren, Anais, Candace and Arianna, were the complete package of beauty, brains, sophistication and hustle. With the exception of Anais, we all graduated from FSU. Lauren received her degree in engineering and worked as a surveyor; Candace graduated with her degree in business with a minor in chemistry and had her own cosmetics line. Arianna finished with a bachelor's in political science and was currently working for a congressman. And yours truly held a bachelor of science in nursing and was currently employed as a pediatric nurse at Mercy Hospital.

Even though we had amazing careers and made great money, we still had our hustle, which involved getting with the man of our dreams and living that jet set, fairy tale life. Candace was lucky enough to find hers, and we all had to catch up. We looked at Miami Fashion Week Swim as the landscape for us to continue our hunt. We knew the after parties would be lit, and we were guaranteed entry to Anais's. As I tried to forget about the note in the limo, Lauren turned to me.

"This is everything!" she exclaimed.

I smiled back at her as the lights dimmed. "It really is," I replied.

All eyes were on the stage as the soca music began to play in the background. Each model was tall and lithe with golden brown skin and thigh gaps, and they sashayed down the runway to Machel Montano. Anais, being the bajan princess that she was, never failed to represent where she came from, and tonight she took it to the next level. Her whole collection was a tribute to the Caribbean. I spotted a few pieces that I knew I would have to get the hook up on for next year.

As the last model came out, we all stood up and clapped while Anais appeared on the stage and sashayed out onto the catwalk. My beautiful bestie was a vision in the red Oscar De La Renta eyelet cross over dress and red Giuseppe Zanotti cruel summer sandals. The night was about to begin.

When the show was over and everyone left the tent, the girls and I waited for Anais. She came running toward us. After kisses and greetings were exchanged, she looked at all of us and smiled.

"What did you think of the show?" she asked.

"It was amazing," Arianna replied, and gave her another hug. "We are so proud of you."

"So which one of these suits you gonna let us rock ahead of time?" Lauren asked, teasingly.

Anais laughed. "Girl, I'll make you something one of a kind that no other bitch in Miami will have."

"I like that sound of that!" Lauren exclaimed.

"I know what you're about to ask. Where are the after parties? Well I gotta finish up here, but there are quite a few soirees going on around the hotel. The more exclusive ones, you gotta have an invite too. I'm going to work on that. But for now, I gotta clean up shop. Go have fun. Mix, mingle. When I'm done, I'll text and I'll meet you guys there."

"Okay, mamas," I said as I kissed her cheek. "Don't be too long."

"I won't," Anais responded before going back behind the stage. As we walked outside of the tent and toward the main corridor, a young woman in a body-con dress handed me a thick, shimmering envelope. I looked down at the envelope then back up at the girl.

"You've been personally invited. You and your girls. The limo is waiting for you at the front."

As she walked away, I opened up the letter. Inside was a three-sentence paragraph and a hashtag.

W Hotel, Julio Iglesias Jr.

and Me.

I hope you had time to… #LearnUP

We walked to the front of Collins Park where the limo was waiting for us. The driver opened the door for us as we approached the car. We got in and drove off. I continued to let the girls think that it was Anais who had planned this out for us. As we rode to the W Hotel, I racked my brain, trying to figure out who planned all of this. In my 24 years of life in Miami, I had dated plenty of ballers. Some of them were genuinely good guys, while others were just there for a good time. With those, I got what I could out of them, one being a year of rent covered for me while I was at FSU, and left them in the dust. Needless to say, some of the not so good ones were not used to being on the receiving end of being played, and stalked me or otherwise tried to set me up. I was usually too smart for them, but now with all of this and even involving my girls had me on edge.

We finally reached the W Hotel. As we walked inside toward the venue, the bouncer smiled at us. "Right this way, Ms. Torres," he said as he pulled back the velvet rope and let us in. One of the hostess, a tall, tanned blond, walked up to us.

"Mr. Adams has been expecting you and your guests. He knows that Ms. Marchan will be a little bit late, but she will also be let in VIP as soon as she arrives. I will show you to your table."

I nodded my head. "Okay. Thank you," I said. As the hostess led us up the stairs toward the VIP section, I tried to recall if I knew a Mr. Adams. The only person that came to mind was my tenth grade biology teacher, but I knew he couldn't afford to put me up on anything. He was cute, but he drove a Toyota Camry and although I was only 15 at the time, I was laser focused on the criteria a man would have to fit to date me. Driving a 10-year-old Camry wasn't one of them. As we made our way to the table, I tried to find out who Mr. Adams was. However, all we found was an array of chocolate covered berries with bottles of Havana Club Maximo, Salon Blanc de Blancs Le Mesnil-sur-Oger, orange juice, coke and cranberry juice waiting for us.

Arianna walked over to one of the bottles and picked it up. Her eyes widened as she read the labels. "There must be over 5,000 dollars worth of alcohol here!" she exclaimed, while reaching for a glass.

"If I knew Anais had it like that, I would've have asked for help with these student loans," Lauren said while laughing. She sat down and poured herself a glass of wine. I stood and looked at the ground below as they danced. It was a typical Miami scene, with beautiful women and rich men dancing, fucking on the dance floor and getting high at the VIP tables. I was still searching for this Mr. Adams, but no one made a move or even came up to where we were. About thirty minutes later, I received a text message. I looked down at my phone. It was Anais. She said she was downstairs at the lobby and to come and meet her.

"Anais is here," I said to the girls. They nodded at me as they enjoyed their rum and mimosas. I walked downstairs and spotted Anais as I made my way to the front of the club. She was speaking to the same blond hostess who turned and began to lead her my way. Just as I was about to reach her, a strong arm grabbed me and pushed me against the wall. He caressed my face and before I could scream, he kissed me.

"Did you learn about me?" he whispered against my lips.

I pushed him away, my chocha tingling.

"Who are you and how did you know where I live, where my friends lived and where I would be going?"

"Shh," Mr. Adams said as he put his fingers to my lips and pulled me out of the corner. We made our way through the club to the backstage where the artists were preparing for their performances. He pulled me into a small dressing room and sat me down on the couch. I was finally able to get a good look at him, and I realized he was the gorgeous man I had seen at the beach earlier that day. He was dressed in a well-tailored suit, and watched as my eyes perused him slowly.

"Saville Row. Designed just for me. Just the way you like it," He responded.

"I do," I said.

He smiled at me and took my hand, kissing it. "So did you learn up?" he asked.

Swallowing hard, I said, "I learned that you can get a lot of information from me after spending no more than five minutes with me."

He winked at me. "I get what I want because I run things, like Miami, New Jersey, and pretty soon, New York will king me too. I wanted you, and since I could tell you're not a girl that is easily impressed, I knew I had to do something to get your attention. You may not know me Ms. Torres, but I've known about you for a couple years now and just wanted to choose the right time to make you mine."

"Is that right, chulo?" I said, raising my eyebrow.

"It is. By the end of the night, you will belong to me." He looked down in between my legs and his eyes raised up to my breasts and lingered there.

"I want to know what all that tastes like and feels like."

I felt my body tingle again.

"We're gonna watch Julio perform from here. Don't worry. Your girls will be alright, but you're spending the rest of the night with me."

"Okay," I said with trepidation. I was all for commanding men. Alpha males were my weakness, but even this was too much for me. However, I stayed put and from our little corner of the club, we watched the show. During that time, I learned that his name was not Mr. Adams, but Ty Martinez, and money was no object to him.

After the party, we cruised in his black on black Maybach to the SLS hotel where I spent the rest of my night in the villa penthouse with my legs wrapped around Ty. I awoke in the morning to a bottle of champagne and orange juice, with a vegetable omelet and berry filled crepes. I initially thought I was alone because Ty was nowhere to be found, but as my senses adjusted to my surroundings, I heard the shower running and saw the steam coming from the open door that led to the bathroom. I sat up in the bed as he turned the shower off. A few minutes later, he came into the bedroom, completely naked and drying off his hair. His gray eyes glowed against his skin. My God, this man was perfecto.

"You're up, mi amor?" he asked as he walked up and planted a gentle kiss on my lips.

I nodded my head and smiled. I must have came at least four times last night. He was a rough but passionate lover—just the way I liked it. I stood up to go to the bathroom and clean myself up when a sudden pain hit me between my thighs. I limped over to the bathroom.

"Good to know I still got it," he said, laughing as he watched me enter the bathroom. "You better get used to this big Dominican dick, Cubana, cause it's yours for life."

"Oh you haven't seen nothing yet, papi. I got you next time," I said as I eased myself down onto the toilet. I took some toilet paper and ran cool water over it before applying it to my bollo.

Ty called out to me. "I can take care of that, chula."

"No, I'm okay," I said, wincing in pain. *I'm so gonna get him back for this.* I thought to myself. And the rest was history.

Two years later, I arrived at our penthouse apartment in South Beach. The two years spent together had been good to us. We had travelled the world and he kept me in the dopest fashions. He was also faithful. We talked about taking it to the next level many times. He said he would proceed when he reached the status that he needed to reach.

Although I knew about what my man did, he kept it away from me in case he got into trouble. He told me several times that he didn't want to be the cause of my downfall. But as time went on, I began to get more worried. When he would go on his missions, he always made sure to be back in two days tops, but now, he stayed gone for at least a week at a time. Even though the trips were beautiful and I would find myself in Santorini or Monaco, I wanted to settle down with my man and not have to worry anymore.

Things had been getting a little tense at home, but it was nothing that we couldn't get through. He was the only man who was able to tame me, and I was the only one who understood him. We would get through this and it would be smooth sailing. I parked my Mercedes truck in my parking space and took the bags out of the car. He gave me free reign to spend and I didn't disappoint. Chanel, Louboutin and Zanotti got a good fifteen thousand out of me today. I walked into our apartment. It was quiet inside.

"Alo? I called out. There was no answer. I put the bags down near the door and walked through the living room toward the back of our loft.

I turned into Ty's office and there he was with another one of his "boys." As I stood at the doorway about to walk in, Ty's voice stopped me.

"I thought I told you to stay out until I called you to come back home," he said with venom in his voice.

"But baby, I'm finished. I—"

"I gave you 20,000 dollars. That should have lasted you a couple hours."

"But I.—"

Ty looked to the man to his left. "We'll finish this tomorrow, Beto."

Beto nodded and walked out of the room. He gave me a once-over before he left the room. I saw Ty's eyes darken as he nodded his head. Beto was in trouble. A couple minutes later, we heard the door open and shut. Ty stared straight at me as I walked into the room.

"Baby, I just missed you, that's all. That's why I wanted to come back," I said.

Ty put up his hand shushing me. He narrowed his eyes at me. "It's about what the fuck I say, not how the fuck you feel. Your ass wanna get caught up, don't you? You won't be happy until you do. I might just let you."

"But I——" I cried.

"But nothing. How you think I keep you laced? You think you can get this on a nine to five? I knew you was crazy, it's part of your charm, but I didn't know you was stupid."

I paused and ran up to him, standing directly in front of him, spitting venom. "Nigga, you think I'm stupid? I know why you do what you do. You already know how hard you gotta work to keep this and I admire that you do. But face it nigga, I keep my own dough, while you risk your life to keep me in Chanel. I got you wrapped around this," I screamed as I put my pinkie up in the air.

Ty looked down and nodded his head. The next thing I knew, my head was rocked back as he slapped me across the face. Before I was able to completely recover, he slammed me up against the wall, holding me by my throat. With his lips barely grazing my ear, he whispered, "How you know that when I'm not with you, I ain't smashing five to ten other bitches? Hay tres mujeres a las que se podrían cambiar por y serían felices con su posición. Don't forget that. You can be replaced." He then let me go and caressed my cheek. "Now go lay down," he said.

I held the tears back and walked out of the room. I went to our guest room and locked the door behind me. As I laid down on the bed, I let the tears spill. Ty had never hit me, ever. There were a lot of things that I overlooked with that man, but this was something I couldn't handle. I wouldn't allow it. The man that I loved, the one who I thought I would marry, did something he knew he wasn't allowed to do, but he just had to show his power over me. After this situation, I was no longer his woman. I became his property. No matter how fine he was, how much money he made, and all the other times he made me feel good, I couldn't allow this to happen. It happened once, and I knew it would happen again. The pillow was wet with my tears. I turned to my side and cried myself to sleep.

I woke up in the morning in my own bed. Ty was staring at me. As I sat up, he leaned forward in the bed and kissed my forehead. "I love you," he said, and got up. He left the room, closing the door behind him.

I showered and went downstairs. On the kitchen counter were two bands of money and some flowers. Ty walked up to me and kissed me gently on the lips. "This will never happen again. And to ensure this, you have free reign of the house, and I will be handling business somewhere else. You have my number. I'll be available, mi amor. I'll be home before sundown."

I simply nodded my head and smiled at him.

"Enjoy your breakfast, baby," Ty said as he gave me one more kiss and left. I stood there as I heard his footsteps go down the hallway. Now it was my time to make my move. Walking slowly back into the bedroom, I pulled out my luggage and frantically packed up about a week's worth of outfits. I had no idea where I was going to go, but I knew I had to leave here. After I finished packing my last items, I quickly ran outside to see if Ty had come back. The coast was still clear. I came back into the room and dialed Candace's number on my phone. After the second ring, I heard that familiar voice.

"Hey boo. What's up?" Candace said.

"I need to come and see you," I said, trying to keep my voice calm.

"Hell froze over?" she said with concern in her voice.

"Yes. It did," I nodded while wiping my eyes.

"Come on through. I'll be there."

I hung up the phone.

I never thought I would ever leave Miami for an extended period of time, but I knew I had to get the hell away from Ty's crazy ass. I took out my laptop and booked the quickest flight out to Jersey. I flew business class, using my own personal card. I called my boss to let her know I would be out on a family emergency and would be returning within the next two weeks. The cool thing about being a nurse was that I worked per diem and I could take off as much as time as I wanted to. I might need more than that, depending on what my final decision would be concerning Ty.

Making sure that I had everything together, I ordered an Uber and walked out of my apartment, locking the door behind me. I made my way outside and into the car. Usually I made small talk with the driver as we made our way to the destination, however this time, I just kept my eyes closed and plotted as we drove to the airport. After 30 minutes, I arrived at my terminal and went to the self-help kiosk to print out my ticket. I was already pre-TSA approved so I went through the line quickly. After my security screening, I set myself up at a restaurant and ordered a few drinks.

I paid attention to my time. It was T-minus one hour until I left Miami for New Jersey. I was blessed to at least have somewhere to go. I knew it would be easy to trace me if I went to a hotel, and I couldn't chance that. I would tell my parents and family where I was once I was settled, but for now, it was just get out of Miami as fast as I could. I texted Candace as I sipped on my sex on the beach.

"I'm on the way. I'll see you in two hours. I took Delta."

Candace replied back. "Okay, I'll see you soon. XOXO. Safe flight."

Forty-five minutes later, business class was allowed to board the plane. I picked up my two carry-ons and made my way to the front of the line. As I was being seated in the plane, I took out my Beats by Fendi and my iPhone and let the soothing sounds of Maxwell drift me off to sleep. As I felt the plane back out of its gate, the voice of the captain came on.

"Welcome to Delta Airlines."

I let out a deep sigh. Today was the start of my new life.

CHAPTER 2

I did my best to hold back the tears as I flew to Jersey. I was only able to visit Candace a few times since she had moved up there to be with her new husband. Each time I visited, she was up there alone. It seemed as if her husband was never at home. I was too busy studying for the NCLEX and interviewing for potential job offers to get up there often. On multiple occasions, we had a conversation that always ended up with Candace begging me to move up there with her. She didn't know anyone and I knew it was kind of hard for her to make friends. I remembered the first conversation like it was yesterday.

We sat at our favorite restaurant, Zanders.

She had met her husband, Zerek, about four months before, and through a whirlwind courtship filled with trips to Paris and Milan, she accepted his marriage proposal. As she was showing me the insanely large pink diamond that rested on her well-manicured left ring finger, she asked me to do the unacceptable.

"Come with me to Jersey."

I looked up at her. "Sure, I can visit for a couple days. It's nothing," I answered.

"No. I mean stay with me. Like for good. Zee has plenty of money and you can either stay with us or we can put you up in one of his apartments until you get on your feet. Plus, there's plenty of ballers—"

"There's plenty of ballers here too, plus sun and sand and—"

"Kiki, I don't know any one up there and you know how hard it is for me to make friends," she pleaded.

I took a deep breath. "You can't convince him to stay here?" I asked. I felt my girl's pain but honestly, I was trying to get where she was. She had it all: the beauty, the brains, the job and now the handsome, rich husband. She really lucked up, and she lucked up in Miami. I felt that I could do the same there, too.

Candace rolled her eyes and put her head in her hands. "I tried!" she groaned. "But it didn't make a difference. Everything he has is in Jersey." She then turned and looked at me. "It would be easier for me to up and leave than him."

I understood. These were the sacrifices that had to be made when you met the perfect one. To be honest, I wasn't sure what I would do if I was in the same situation. I looked up at Candace and smiled. "I'll come visit as much as possible. Who knows? Maybe one day, something may happen that will make me move from Miami. And Jersey or wherever you will be at the time will be the first place I come to."

Fighting back tears, Candace looked up at me and laughed. "The only way I can see that happening is if Hell freezes over."

I laughed. "You know me so well."

We surprised Candace with an all-expense paid bachelorette party in Honolulu. Over those three days, we spent the days sunning on the white sand beaches and spent our nights clubbing in the VIP section. On our last night of our trip as we sat in the penthouse of the Modern Honolulu Hotel, over mimosas and loud, we quizzed Candace on all things wedding and Zerek.

"So how did you guys officially meet?" Lauren asked.

"Well, I was at Whole Foods, standing in line, and I felt someone tap me on the shoulder." She proceeded to give us every detail from there.

Candace's destination wedding in the Bahamas was the stuff legends were made of. Everyone who was invited had all of their expenses paid. As I walked down the aisle with Candace's older brother, Mike, I was glad to see that one of my girls was living the dream. I was jolted out of my memory of that special day by the plane's captain.

"We are entering into New Jersey airspace. Ladies and gentlemen, as we start our descent, please make sure your seat backs and tray tables are in their full upright position. Make sure your seat belt is securely fastened and all carry-on luggage is stowed underneath the seat in front of you or in the overhead bins. Thank you."

I looked out of the window and watched our

descent into EWR airport. It looked so gray and murky down there. It was nothing like my beautiful Miami with its white, shimmering beaches and golden high-rise towers. I didn't know how I was going to fit in. I still didn't understand how Candace did it. We finally landed with a slight bounce and the pilot slowed up the plane as we approached the gate.

"Ladies and gentlemen, welcome to Newark Liberty International Airport. Local time is 3:20pm, and the temperature is 75 degrees."

Seventy-five degrees? No comprendo! I thought to myself.

The captain continued his landing speech as the plane finally stopped and the seat belt light was turned off. People started getting up and pulling their luggage from the overhead compartment. I did the same and made my way out of the plane. As I walked down the jet bridge with my Goyard roller case and purse, I took out my phone and dialed Candace.

"You're here boo?" she asked excitedly over the line.

"Yes, I'm in Jersey," I replied.

"Do you need to get your luggage or did you carry everything on the plane?"

"I have everything. You can just come and get me."

"Okay, I'll be there in about ten minutes. Delta terminal?"

"Delta terminal," I repeated.

"See you then."

I hung up the phone and entered the airport, following the directions to ground transportation. Lo and behold, out of the sea of Toyotas and Kias, a beautiful all white Maybach pulled up in front of me. Candace always made an entrance wherever she went, and today she didn't disappoint. My girl got out of the car, dressed to the nines in Balmain and Dolce and Gabbana. Her Pigalles matched the exact brown of her skin. Her hair was cut in an asymmetrical bob that was curled at the end. As she approached me to hug me, I noticed something different about her face that I couldn't quite put my finger on. She pulled back from me and gave me the once-over while holding my shoulders.

"Girl, you look too good," she said, smiling.

"Girl you too. I'm so happy to see you still got that Miami swag."

"You can take the girl out the hood but you

can't take the hood out the girl," she replied, laughing.

"So this can be home?" I asked.

Candace sighed and walked toward her car. "You can make home anywhere," she said.

I put my luggage into her trunk and got in the car. We sped off. As usual, soca music was playing in the background as we navigated our way out of the busy airport. It was a Thursday and that always tended to be a busy travel day. When we were finally on the interstate, she turned down the music and smiled.

"I'm so excited that my bestie is staying up here for a while. It will be a little less lonely."

"Don't tell me that you still don't have any friends? You've been up here for almost two years. No excuses," I said.

She rolled her eyes and it was then that I finally noticed what the difference was. Candace had started wearing green eye contacts. I never knew her to have an eye problem. I'd known Candace was for almost 15 years and I never once saw her wear glasses or anything. I guess she wanted to try something new. It looked good on her.

"Girl, have you seen these Jersey bitches?

Leopard print and aqua net hair gel. No thank you."

"That's mean. Maybe you can be an inspiration."

"How about no?"

I laughed. "Well now you got me."

"Finally. So where do you want to eat?" Candace asked.

"I feel like a steak," I replied.

"What type? Bistek?"

I looked at her in mock disgust. "Chica. Please."

"Filet mignon it is."

I winked at her.

We pulled up to a place called Steakhouse 85. From looking at the surroundings, I knew we would make quite an entrance. We got out of the car and walked inside. We were seated immediately and handed menus. After we placed our orders, Candace put her drink menu down and stared at me.

"So, hell froze over huh?"

"Colder than a nun's crotch," I replied.

"So what happened?" she asked.

I took a deep sigh and swallowed hard. I didn't want to cry in public. I looked at

Candace. "It's been building up, and finally he just snapped. You know, I just don't understand Ty. Whenever he's doing his little bit of dirt, he sends me out with some money and tells me to buy up South Beach. I do just that with the girls and come home late, then he flips crazy and accuses me of cheating. Now I'm many things, Candace. I can be sneaky, I can be conniving, and I don't let nothing get in the way of what I want—"

"And that's why we love you," Candace responded, laughing.

"But one thing I'm not is a cheater. Then when I come home early, he gets mad because I didn't wait until he called. I missed him and wanted to come home. Most times, he's sweet, but yesterday he took it to the next level. He hit me and—"

Candace's eyes widened and her jaw set in anger. "What? Girl we can get this handled!" she exclaimed as she reached for her phone.

I put my hand on her phone. "That's a war I'm not ready to fight," I said.

Candace put her phone back on the table.

I continued, "He acted so normal, like nothing happened. After he told me he could replace me with three bitches, and then acted like nothing happened. I couldn't do it anymore. This was a man I wanted to marry, but I can't."

Candace reached down and grabbed my hand, squeezing it. "You can stay here with me as long as you need to."

"Thank you," I said, choking back tears.

"You're lucky you got that nursing degree. You can get a job anywhere."

"I know I am. I don't think I'll be here that long to even worry about that."

"Well, I'm just putting it out there."

"I saw how you slid that in there," I said laughing.

CHAPTER 3

The Maybach drove so smooth that it lulled me to sleep. When I awoke about thirty minutes later, we were pulling up to Candace's amazing mansion. She had just moved in about three months ago. When she said the place was fit for royalty, I thought she was exaggerating, but now that I was seeing it first hand, I could see she was definitely telling the truth.

We pulled up to a wrought iron gate accented with brick posts. Candace reached up and pressed the top of her sun visor and the gates swung inward. Candace drove inside. Leading up to her house was a beautiful, vibrant, green lawn that seemed to go on for miles and led to a roundabout driveway with a water fountain in the center. My mouth dropped open as we finally approached her home. It was a large brick affair with white columns and shutters. The house seemed to be as long as a Miami block. We finally parked near the front door.

Candace turned to me and winked. "So what do you think?" she asked. I continued to stare in awe at this beautiful mansion. Although it was New Jersey, Miami didn't have shit on this. Candace and Zerek were only dating for a few months when they got engaged and married. She just told us that he was cakin' and that he gave her anything her heart desired. She wasn't playing.

We pulled to the front of the house where two servants were waiting. They walked over to the car and opened the doors for us. I turned to Candace, my face betraying my surprise and slight envy over her life. I turned around as the butler brought in my luggage and closed the door behind us. Candace pointed him into the direction of a gorgeous spiraling staircase in the middle of a sumptuous living room. All white furniture with turquoise and golden yellow accents. The place was laid.

"Do you want a tour?" Candace asked.

I shook my head no. "I just wanted to lay down for a while. I'm tired."

Candace smiled at me, excited.

"This was bought on a dare," she said to me as we walked inside the mansion.

"What did you dare him to do?" I asked, incredulously.

She shrugged as she walked through the door. "Zee dared me. He asked me to find the biggest home he could buy with cash and he would do just that. So we went house hunting and I came upon this beauty. The going price for this place was around twenty million dollars. He was ready to buy the place on the spot. A few weeks later, we were sitting in the realtor's office as he signed over a check for over twenty-two million dollars. I didn't know what to say after that."

I just continued to stare at the luxury around me in awe. It was almost overwhelming.

"You must be tired. I've never known you to be quiet for too long," Candace said and smiled at me. I nodded. "Let me show you to your room."

We went up the spiral staircase and up to the

spacious loft style family room area complete with a 70-inch flat screen TV and white leather couches and love seats. We went down two doors before Candace threw one open and ushered me in. I walked into a brilliantly lit, all white bedroom that was the size of a small apartment. The decor was art deco with splashes of turquoise and yellow as accessories. A Cali king platform bed with white leather headboard stood in the middle, overlooking the balcony with a view of the large backyard and Jersey City in the distance. I looked through each drawer and saw that the butler had already folded and neatly put away my clothes. I then walked over to the balcony and looked at the small house to the right.

"You like it?" Candace asked me, smiling.

"I do!" I exclaimed.

"See what I told you? You should've come and visit. I wasn't going to have you out of your comfort zone," she said laughing.

She walked over to another door and turned to me. "Kiki, let me show you your bathroom." I followed her into a bathroom that looked like it was straight out of *Better Homes and Gardens*.

I've never seen a bathroom like this outside of a magazine. It was bigger than some people's bedrooms. Skylights provided light to the room, and there was a spa tub in the middle of the room and a marble shower with two shower-heads that were positioned on each side. I could definitely get used to this.

Candace turned to me and smiled. "If you want to freshen up, you can."

"I'm fine," I responded. We walked back toward the bedroom. I plopped down on the bed and looked at Candace, who sat in one of the leather chaise lounges near the balcony.

"So you think you can make this work for a few months?" she asked.

I shrugged my shoulders. "Meh, it will do," I said, smiling.

"I'm just so happy you're here. These Jersey girls are too much. There's nothing like having your best friend here with you. You can take all the time you need until you get situated."

I simply nodded in response. "It shouldn't take that long.

"So, you're not going back to him? Right?" She questioned.

My eyes widened as I sat up. I didn't really know how to approach the situation with Tyron and me. I didn't know if I wanted to hear the "I told you so's" at this moment. Candace knew I had a thing for the bad boys, and sometimes you have to deal with those consequences when you are fucking with one. I knew the reason why she asked, but I didn't want to be lectured. All I wanted to do honestly was sleep. But since Candace was my best friend, I thought I would tell her just a little something. I sighed as she walked over to the bed and sat next to me.

"Well, I will put it to you like this for now. I love him, and I know I'm a whole lot to handle, and I can handle a whole lot too, but Tyron was just too much and I couldn't take it anymore. I like it rough, but not that rough."

Candace's face fell as she listened to me. Her eyebrows furrowed as she put her hand up to shush me. "But he hit you, Kiki!" she exclaimed, angrily.

I looked down and then back up at her. "That is all I have to say about the situation."

She looked at me skeptically. I just smiled at her.

"Let's lighten this up. How are things going

with the LustLavishly Line? Girl, I am so proud of you. I think I came at the right time too, because I just ran out of the Copper rose lip gloss you sent me."

Candace laughed and shrugged. "Girl, I sent you four tubes of that."

"Last November, and when you wear it every day, you're bound to run out."

"I'll see what I can do." She winked at me and continued, "Well, as of September, we will be in Sephora and Ulta Stores, plus we're working on getting someone very famous to be the face of the line."

I clapped my hands together and squealed. "Girl, I knew you could do it. I will be telling everybody about your line. Who is the famous face?" I asked as I pushed her gently on the arm.

"I can't disclose that information but she is one of the baddest in the modeling game. And I don't mean that club hosting, former stripper bullshit. I mean Milan and Paris Runway, ten thousand dollars a walk type chick. That should give you a clue."

Like with her wedding, house and every-thing else in her life, Candace always took it to the next level. But I wouldn't have her any other way. You had to be extra if you were going to be in my inner circle. I still had the events of the previous few days in my head and I knew that she would find another way to find out what happened, so I decided to ask her some more questions so she wouldn't pry too much into my life.

"So, I mean I've seen the shows, Jersey Shore and Mob Wives. Please tell me that there is more to do out here than what I saw on TV?"

Candace's eyes wandered toward the ceiling as she thought about all the fun things to do. She stayed looking that way for a few minutes. My heart completely sank. She then looked back at me, smiling helplessly.

"Well, we have Atlantic City and the Jersey Shore, but I say we just live it up in Manhattan. We aren't that far from there."

I nodded and laughed. "I can do Manhattan."

Candace grabbed my hands and smiled at me. "I'm so happy to have a genuine friend to do things with and share my life out here. Please stay as long as you need."

"Chica, from the looks of things, you may never get rid of me."

We both laughed until we heard the footsteps coming up the spiral staircase. A deep voice called out. "Candy, you home babe?"

Candace smiled and blushed slightly. "Zee is here. I'll let him know you're here."

We both got out of the bed and walked toward the family room. I paused as I caught a full glimpse of him. I remembered him from the wedding a few years ago, but I didn't remember him being this damn fine. Shit. He was an easy 6'2" with smooth, caramel skin, and he was built like a god. I bit my lower lip, but instinctively covered it up to ensure that no one, especially Candace, could detect my instant desire for him.

She ran up and gave him a kiss, then turned and motioned for me to come toward them. I walked over slowly, trying to keep my eyes focused on his gorgeous, piercing, light brown eyes.

"Zee, this is the friend that is going to stay with us for a while. You remember Kiyana, don't you?"

Zerek smiled at me, flashing flawless, pearly-white teeth and deep dimples.

"I believe I do. You were the maid of honor if I recall. Long time, no see, sis. Good to see you brought some sunshine back into my wife's life." Zerek extended his hand to me and as I shook it, I felt electricity run through my body. I had thoughts of how his hands would feel caressing my body. I immediately shook the thoughts out of my head.

"Nice to see you again. We'll take good care of you," he continued as he let go of my hand.

I nodded. "Nice to see you again also."

Zerek turned to Candace and smiled. "Did you give her a tour of the house?"

Candace smiled and turned back to me. "Yes, I did."

"Where did you place her?"

"In the other bedroom, down the hallway."

"Well babe, if she's going to be here for a while, why don't we just put her up in one of the guest homes?"

Candace pouted a little bit but then cheered back up. "I thought she wanted to be a little bit closer to me, but knowing my girl, she likes her privacy. I'll have Ronald repack her stuff and move to the guest house." She turned back to me. "Let's give you the full tour."

We walked downstairs and through the living room to the kitchen. The floor and counters were a cream marble with large, golden and turquoise swirls. The walls were cream with sandalwood cabinets. All of the appliances with stainless steel. At the back of the kitchen, there was a large balcony that led to the backyard that was lush with plenty of fruit trees. I remembered how much Candace loved to cook and make her own desserts, so I knew this would be paradise for her. About a hundred feet away from the main house was a small cottage. We walked up the path and opened the door. It was the size of an apartment, with leather couches, a flat screen TV, stainless steel kitchen appliances and a gorgeous bedroom.

Candace smiled at me and said, "You'll definitely have more privacy here, in case you decide to have a visitor or two."

I winked at her. Candace definitely knew me. I glanced over at Zerek for a moment. I wouldn't mind if he paid me a visit.

Zerek walked back over to Candace and put his arm around her waist. "Well, make yourself at home. Candace and I would like to take you out to dinner. We can go to the city if you would like. She told me about how you have certain requirements as to where you eat."

As he said that last line, his eyes momentarily lingered at my waist. I felt my body tingle under his gaze. I just smiled at him. "After I freshen up, sure. Thank you."

Candace nodded at me. She followed Zerek out of the living room, shutting the door behind her. I collapsed on the couch and knocked out. By the time I woke up again, it was around 9:30p.m. I looked at my cell phone. Candace sent me a text message.

"We can reschedule for tomorrow night. I know you went through a lot and you're tired. I'm so happy you're here. I'm gonna prove to you that Jersey got it. I love you mamas and see you in the morning."

I smiled and got up, walking to the bedroom. I laid down in the big king size bed. As I laid on my back staring at the ceiling, my thoughts floated back to Zerek. My body had never really reacted to a man the way it did when I saw him. I'd dealt with some fine ass men in my life, and ones with money too, but Zerek was next level. I knew that was my girl's husband and she was a good woman, but damn this was hard. I had always respected the girl code, but there were exceptions to every rule. I would never come on to him, but if he did come after me, I wouldn't turn it down. A girl has needs, and at the moment, Zerek was what I needed.

CHAPTER 4

I tossed and turned in my bed all night. In my dreams, I felt the heat and weight of a man on top of me. His caresses were rough and passionate. I felt the rough wetness of a tongue across my nipples, making its way down my stomach towards my—

I was all of sudden jolted out of my sleep, super wet. I couldn't see his face, but I knew who he was. My ability to keep up the girl code was dissolving by the minute. It hadn't even been a full day and I was already sweating.

I got out of bed and walked into the bathroom, planning on taking a shower to cool myself off. I tied up my hair and undressed, then turned on both of the showerheads and

stepped inside. There were also four mini showerheads that gave a massaging effect on my back
and shoulders. A chica could definitely get used
to this.

After my long hot shower, I dried myself off
on the plush white towels and went into my
room to pick out my outfit. I only brought a
week's worth of clothes with me, and I knew I
would have to eventually go shopping. I saw
how they dressed in New Jersey and it was safe
to say that I would either be hitting up
Manhattan or online shopping for my clothes. I
looked outside to judge the weather and then
glanced at my phone for confirmation. Today
would be around 75 degrees, so I pulled out my
cream-colored halter dress with gold gladiator
sandals. After adding some coconut oils to my
curls and putting on some lip-gloss, I was ready
for breakfast. I secretly hoped Zerek would be
home as I walked out of the guest cottage
toward the main house.

As I approached, I caught a glimpse of
Zerek as he was making coffee. I allowed myself
a moment to admire him from afar, while he
prepared breakfast. He was wearing a pair of
dark blue jeans with a wife-beater. I watched as

his golden brown muscles flexed as he chopped up fruit and put it into a bowl. I bit my lower lip again as I walked through the double doors and into the kitchen. He turned around and smiled at me as I walked towards the island and sat down on one of the stools.

"So how was your first night here?" he asked me.

"I slept wonderfully," I answered coyly.

"That's good," he said. "So how did you meet Candace? She's told me so much about you, but I want to hear your side of the story." He winked at me.

It would only be a matter of time, I thought to myself as I prepared my answer. "What did she tell you about me?"

Zerek raised his eyebrow and laughed. "Oh so you wanna know how to work your story? Leave out all the juicy parts huh?"

I laughed. "Something like that," I replied.

"Well I will say this. Candace has nothing but amazing things to say about you. Out of all her girls, you were the one she talked about the most. I know we didn't really get a chance to get to know each other while I was dating her, but time waits for no man or woman. So I kind of feel like I'm meeting you for the first time. Where are you from originally?"

I licked my lips and answered, "Well, my family is from Cuba, but I was born in Miami."

Zerek turned to me and smiled. "Miami, you say? That's my second home. They got the best of everything, especially the women." I felt my body soften when he said that. "In fact," he continued, "I have some serious connections there, especially in South Beach."

"South Beach you say. I know all the heavy hitters. Let me see who you know," I said, winking at him.

He turned to me and smiled. He gave me the onceover. "You probably do. You most definitely would be their type."

"Glad to see you're finally up," Candace's voice echoed. I turned around as she walked into the kitchen. She ran over to Zerek, giving him a quick kiss on the lips, and sat down next to me. "I hope you got some rest."

I smiled at her. "I did. Plenty."

"Good," she replied. She turned to Zerek and smiled as he handed her a plate of waffles, poached eggs and fruit. Pouring herself a glass of orange juice, she continued, "Zee and I finally have a day off to ourselves. So we're going to be gone for a while. You have full access to the house. Make yourself at home."

Zerek handed me a plate and I dug in. He sat next to Candace and across from me. He had a protein shake and a plate of eggs and fruit. I loved a man who could take care of himself.

"So what did I miss?" Candace asked, as she took a sip of her orange juice.

"I was just telling her that we may know some people in common in Miami."

"You probably do," Candace answered. She then turned to me and smiled. "So like I said, the house is yours and if you need a car to get around, you can take my Audi. I trust you with it."

I smiled. "Thanks for opening up your home to me, both of you, at such short notice. I totally understand needing to get away for a while. Hell, that's what I did. I'll probably spend the day looking for new jobs. I know there must be some hospitals hiring."

Zerek smiled at me. "Plenty. I can also put in a good word for you too. I'll ask around and see what I can come up with."

"Thank you," I replied.

Candace snapped her fingers. "That reminds me." She stood up and scurried away from the kitchen. I tried my best to focus on my food and not Zerek, who began eyeballing me the minute she left the room. If this kept up and Candace wasn't back in time, I knew that I would have my legs wrapped around his head. I could only imagine all of the things he would do to me.

Candace returned shortly afterward with two sets of keys in her hands. She set them on the table next to my plate and pointed to the set of four keys with the Gucci key ring. "These are the spare house keys. I had these made for you when we first moved in. I'm happy that you're finally able to use them." She then pointed to the second set, one lone key on a Hermes key ring. "This one is for the Audi. Have fun."

I looked down at the keys and smiled. I then snuck another glance at Zerek. Oh, I knew I would. "Thank you for everything."

Candace smiled at me. "That's what best friends do." Zerek leaned over and kissed her on the forehead.

"I'll let Thomas know to get our things

together," he said. He then turned to me and smiled. "It was good talking to you, Kiyana. We'll finish the convo later."

"Likewise." I replied. Zerek left the room. Candace finished up the last of her breakfast and put the plates in the dishwasher.

She stood up and straightened out her dress, then gave me a quick hug and kiss on the cheek. "Call me if you need me."

"I will." I watched as she left the kitchen and went upstairs. It was going to be a long afternoon.

CHAPTER 5

It was around four thirty when Zerek and Candace were finally ready for their overnight rendezvous. Candace revealed to me that Zee rented the Ty Warner Penthouse suite at the Four Seasons hotel in New York. My mouth dropped open in awe as she told me. You had to book that room at least a year in advance and it ran upwards of 35,000 dollars a night. I'd had men wine and dine me to no end, but this man was beyond. They didn't make too many of them. It was getting harder and harder to maintain my cool.

I waved good-bye as I watched them walk hand in hand out the door from the foyer. They got into their Maybach and I watched them round the corner and drive out of the gate, ready to spend the night with one another. I shut the door behind me and made my way to the guesthouse.

I took my laptop out of the bedroom and walked into the living room. After settling on the couch with a drink in hand, I turned on my laptop and checked out my emails. To my surprise, I saw about ten emails from Ty, telling me he missed me in the subject line. I didn't know how to feel at that point. At first, I found it flattering, because basically, they always wanted me back, but at the same time, I found it weird because I didn't get not one phone call or text message from him. Usually, when men would beg me to give them another chance, they would blow up my phone and use email as a last resort to contact me. Then again, Ty was not the usual nigga. I opened up one of the emails.

"My dearest munequita,

There are many things I want to say to you right now, about how I feel. I didn't contact you for a day or so because I wanted to find the exact words to express the millions of emotions that are flooding through me right now. I just want you to think about the first time I met you, and how without so much as knowing your last name, I was able to find out not only what you were doing later on that night, but where you lived, your friends lived and even what fashion show you were attending.

From that night, without knowing your birthday or what you did for a living, I gave you everything and upgraded you beyond your wildest dreams. So knowing all of this, I don't know where the fuck you get off thinking that I won't find you now. Back then, I fell in love with you at first sight. Your golden skin reminded me of sunshine and your eyes were two shining, precious gems that brought light into my life, but now all I want to do is find you and extinguish you. You are as good as dead and I will be coming for you. You won't be able to hide for long."

I closed the email. I knew he wasn't serious about that. I mean I knew he could be a little dramatic with his shit and we did have our issues, but naw. He couldn't have been serious. He would never hurt me like that. He just missed me and wanted me shook. I opened up another email from him.

"Hermosurita,

Every hour that you are gone stirs a fire in me—one that only you can quench. I miss the scent of your skin and the way you felt against me. Each minute that goes by reminds me of all I did for you and how I need you back here with me. With every second since you left, I have these visions of slitting your throat and watching you take your last breath. I really thought you were something special, which is why I sacrificed everything for you. But like most females, you're only good for one thing, and even that was mediocre. Otherwise, you're worthless. You were wrong for leaving me the way you did, and I'm coming for you. I won't let you know when because I want to keep you on your toes. That will make it that much sweeter.

Azucar"

I read the email over and over again. This nigga was straight loony. I could deal with crazy, but I didn't know about this shit. I had to get my mind off this. I had a new life out here and I had to make it as normal as possible. He wouldn't know where I was because I left the state. Finding where I was in Miami is one thing, but I was at least a thousand miles away from him now. I calmed my breathing down and moved all of those emails out of my inbox.

After moving the ten emails he sent me, and setting up a filter in case he sent more, I opened up a browser and logged on to my Indeed account. I typed in pediatric nurse in Jersey City and surrounding communities. Roughly one hundred jobs popped up. I looked for jobs that paid a minimum of eighty thousand dollars with a flexible schedule. I sorted the jobs by pay and then by date, and began to take down their information. I updated my resume and began to submit my applications. Over the next two hours, I must have submitted at least thirty resumes. I had no worries. I would probably be employed by the end of the week, since I could guarantee at least a fifty percent response rate. Nurses with my experience were hard to come by. I closed my laptop, stood up and stretched.

I looked outside of the window at the main house. I never really got the chance to fully explore their home, so I put on my shoes and walked out of the guest house, toward the mansion. I opened up the sliding door that led to the kitchen and grabbed a peach out of the fruit bowl. I walked out of the kitchen and began to explore. I turned to the left and walked into their dining room. All white table with high backed white chairs on one side and a bench on the other. The cushions were a beautiful shimmering turquoise adorned with golden foil leaves. The table, which could easily sit eight people, was set with bright yellow plates and turquoise bowls placed in the middle. "Hollywood Africans" by Basquiat was the only other piece in the room.

Next, I checked out their laundry room. The room was the size of some people's bedrooms, with a state of the art washer and dryer. On the opposite side of the room was a long silver shelving system with three laundry baskets underneath. It was impressive, but I kept going and soon found the study.

This was the only room that had any air of masculinity to it. The room was dark and rich with mahogany furniture and rows and rows of books that reached up to the cathedral ceiling. The shelf that was eye level to me had a healthy mix of Robert Green, Toni Morrison and Chinua Achebe. As I ran my hand across the books, my hand rested on the Autobiography of Malcolm X. It was one of my favorite books to read. I would have to ask him if I could borrow it sometime.

In the middle of the room stood a large desk with a presidential high backed chair. There was the large state of the art Mac Pro, too. I sat down in the chair and set my phone on the desk.

Next to his cup of Mont Blanc pens were Tiffany-framed photos of him and Candace, including photos of their safaris and their trips to Europe. I couldn't help but feel a little bit jealous of their life. I knew that my girl deserved everything, and I was happy for her, but when was it going to be my turn? I'd had men wine and dine me, but they never seemed to think enough of me to make me a wife. Even with Ty, I was with him for two years, and we moved in together, but he never put a ring on it.

I melted into Zerek's chair and was immediately enveloped into his cologne, Sauvage by Christian Dior. It was one of my favorites. My mind immediately began to wander. I imagined him sitting at the desk, working at his computer when I walked in and quietly shut the door behind me. He looked up at me and smiled as I made my way over to him. He immediately grabbed me and pulled me into his lap. Burying his hands in my curls, he kissed me deeply. I wrapped my hands around his neck as I reciprocated his every movement. While tracing his tongue all over my neck, I threw my head back as he ripped off my shirt and pulled down my bra. I bit my lower lip as his tongue circled my nipple and he pulled it in his mouth. Kissing me again, he suddenly lifted me up and put me on his desk. He pulled my underwear off with his teeth, and began to kiss up my thigh until his lips found my bollo. He looked up at me and smiled.

"I know you taste as good as you look," he said as he lowered his head and started tasting me. I threw my head back as I grabbed the back of his head and began to grind my hips into his face. And I....

"Tell him boy bye...." My ring tone snapped me out of my completely inappropriate thoughts. I looked down at my phone. A New Jersey phone number popped up, so I answered it.

"Kiyana Torres speaking," I answered in my professional voice.

"Hello Ms. Torres. This is Janette Lee with Jersey City Medical Center Pediatric department. We just received your application and we would like to schedule an interview for this upcoming week. We have appointments for next Wednesday and Thursday at 12:30PM and 2:30PM. Let me know your availability?"

I cleared my throat and sat up in the chair. "2:30 on Thursday is perfect."

"Great. I will pencil you in. Thank you, and looking forward to meeting you."

"Likewise," I replied. I hung up my phone. And so it begins.

CHAPTER 6

I had to get myself in tip top form for my interview on Thursday. I kept receiving crazy emails from Ty and I knew the only way to resolve this was for me to sweat it all out. I woke up early the next day and pulled on my leggings and sports bra, ready to head to the on-site fitness room, that was near the pool house.

As with everything else on this property, there were no expenses spared. The room looked like the Miami Spectrum Gym without chicks checking the size of their butt after three squats or dudes trying to hit on me while I was working out. I walked up to the treadmill, which was positioned in front of 55-inch screen TV. I turned on the treadmill and started walking to warm myself up. The TV turned on and instructed me to choose a scene. I always loved the desert, so I chose the Sahara scenic route and adjusted the treadmill to a 1.5 incline at four miles an hour. I put on my headphones and got in my zone.

I felt the thoughts of Ty and his crazy ass melt away from my mind. I sweated out his evil words and beat away the pain each time my feet came in contact with the treadmill. Meek Mill powered me through. Although I kept my focus on the scenery on the TV, out the corner of my eye, I noticed someone standing near the door watching me. Not wanting to lose my stride, I looked towards the right at the mirror, and used the reflection to identify who it was. It was Zerek. He was watching me, looking me up and down, obviously enjoying the view. I felt my body tingle a little bit.

I turned to him without missing a beat and waved at him. He waved back and then left the room. I smiled to myself. Candace was beautiful. She was the true model type, the one that you'd see on the runway. Flawless skin, beautiful brown eyes, and legs that went on for miles. She could even stay svelte, no matter what she ate. I on the other hand was thicker than a Snicker. I had to work out constantly to keep my body on point. Arroz con pollo and mantequilla did give me double D's, and track gave me the Miami booty without the surgery, but I also had to fight to keep my stomach flat.

I guess it was true what they said: broads starve themselves while their men are fucking the fat chick next door. I always noticed the boys married the waif types, the Jackie O's but their mistresses would be the Marilyn Monroe types. I smiled to myself that Zerek found me so attractive. I knew he thought about how I felt in his mind, but I couldn't help but wonder if he would act on those desires. I secretly hoped he would.

That little boost gave me the newfound confidence I needed to tackle my interview. I walked back over to the guesthouse and began to get ready. Before jumping in the shower, I had to pick out the perfect outfit. I chose a cute black skirt suit with ruffled white shirt and killer black heels. I went with the Nine Wests because I learned that when you wore really expensive shoes such as Louboutins or St. Laurent's to an interview actually diminishes your chances of getting the job. Plus, Nine Wests are cute and comfortable, anyway.

I showered quickly and moisturized myself with l'occitane shea butter. While dressed in the plush white guest robe, I took out my Frederic Fekkai straightening balm and flat iron and went to work straightening my hair. Once I was finished, I pulled it back into a long ponytail. I applied a little bit of lip-gloss and highlighter on my cheek and headed for the kitchen. Candace was sitting at the island, eating some cereal. She smiled as I walked through the double doors.

"Where you going looking so fly?" she asked.

"I have a job interview," I answered.

"Already?" she said, astonished.

"Girl, I'm a nurse. I can find a job anywhere," I said, smiling.

"Good luck. I'm rooting for you." She said, squeezing my hand.

"Thanks. I'll let you know how it goes." I picked up the keys to the Audi and walked toward the front room. As I stepped into the car, I typed in the address in Waze and was on my way. Over the last few days since I had arrived in New Jersey, I never really left the house, so this would essentially be my debut in the city. Needless to say, it was drastically different than my beloved Miami. Where Miami was bright, shining with shimmering beaches and turquoise seas, New Jersey was drab and gray, with burnt out buildings. The people just looked—damn. I didn't know how long I would last out here. I hope the sight of children would brighten my mood. I really did love children and hoped to have my own one day.

After about a thirty-minute drive, I finally arrived at my destination. As always, I was ten minutes early. I checked in with the front desk and was directed to the second floor where HR was located. I sat down and prepared myself for the interview. They were all the same. They would ask how many years I had worked with children, how would I handle certain situations such as severe trauma, and so on. I always aced the interviews and my work ethic was incredible. They would be lucky to have me. Sure enough, I met with two older white women, who asked me the same questions, including my favorite, "Why did you leave the last job you had?"

With a smile, I answered like I always did. "I

always look for new opportunities to grow and be challenged."

At the end of the 45-minute interview, they offered me the job at 80,000 a year with a 3,000 dollar bonus. That would be enough for a security deposit and first month's rent on my apartment. I would have to ask Candace where the nice places were later on, because from what I could see, this was just one big slum. I thanked my interviewers and made my way to the car. As I strapped myself in, I called Candace before inputting the address into Waze for the return drive home.

"Hello?" Candace said over the speaker. "How did it go?"

"I start on Monday," I said. "Let's celebrate."

"I'll take you to Manhattan," Candace squealed.

"It's a date," I said and drove off.

When I arrived back at the mansion, Candace already had a Lyft waiting to whisk us off to our Manhattan destination. We got into the back of the Lincoln town car and drove off. She, as usual, was looking like a model, wearing a gorgeous pair of bright blue cigarette pants with a black typical girl t-shirt from Love Moschino, and floral yellow Moschino pumps finishing off the look. She was the only woman I knew who could pull that look off without looking ratchet. She sat next to me in the back-seat, her hair in dark barrel curls and her eyes shining. Candace continued wearing those green contacts. I didn't understand why she wore them, because she had the most beautiful eyes I'd ever seen. They were the color of burnished honey and bore a striking contrast to her smooth tan skin.

"So give me more deets?" Candace asked as we headed toward the bar.

"It's always the same with the hospitals. It's not as exciting as it was when I got my first job." I looked over at her slyly and smiled. "I want to know more about the secret cover girl you have for your line."

She shook her head and smiled. "It's not as exciting as it may sound either." She gently pushed me on my shoulder. "If you buy me enough drinks, I may spill the beans."

I laughed. "Hey, I'm the one looking for the job, not you."

"Yeah, but I have the intel you want too. That doesn't come cheap."

"Bet."

We finally arrived at our destination. I looked up at the unassuming building. I was expecting the glitz of Miami, but was pleasantly surprised to see it packed to the brim with hipsters and Wall Street types alike. It was lit.

"What is the place called?"

"It's called The Dead Rabbit Grocery and Grog. As you can see, it's lit."

We walked into the bar and made our way to the second floor where they had a few unoccupied tables and chairs. We settled ourselves and looked at the menus.

"So, I've been meaning to ask you. Have you heard from Ty?"

The one thing I hated about myself was how my face would always convey what I felt inside. I felt my heart sink and I quickly tried to compose my face, but it was too late. She noticed.

"Nothing. Nothing at all," I replied

"Nuh-uh. I saw that. What's going on?" Candace demanded.

"I've received some emails from him."

"What did they say?"

"That he misses me. He wants to work things out but he said he will give me time before we talk again."

She looked at me, skeptically. "Okay. We have your back if anything else happens. You're not alone in this."

"Thanks," I responded.

The waitress walked up to take our orders. Just in time, I thought to myself.

"Hello ladies. What would you like to drink?" she asked.

"I would like an Empire Club," Candace said.

"And I would like a Tammany Stalwart."

"Coming right up," the waitress said, winking. She left the table.

"Are you hungry?" Candace asked.

"I'm not, but I know you are. I swear I never figured out where you put it."

Sighing, Candace said, wistfully "I wish I could pack it on in all the right spots like you, but God's made us all differently."

The waitress arrived soon with our drinks. They didn't disappoint. We had a couple more drinks before Candace signaled it was time to go.

"Why are we leaving so early?" I asked.

"Got a text from Zerek and I'm not leaving you alone." She pressed a couple buttons on her phone screen and then looked up at me. "The Lyft driver will be here in five minutes. Let's head downstairs." She grabbed my hand and we went downstairs. We pushed through the crowd of people until we made our way to the street.

"What is he driving?" I asked.

"Another Lincoln town car. Don't worry. We won't roll away from here looking like peasants."

The town car arrived about five minutes later and we climbed in. My head was slightly buzzing from all the alcohol. I was used to the margaritas and fruity cocktails from the land of eternal summer known as Miami, but I could get used to the drinks they were serving here in Manhattan too. Getting out of my comfort zone was sometimes a good thing. The drive home was quicker than the drive to the city, and I could see why. There really wasn't too much to do in Jersey.

The driver dropped us off at the front of the house. We walked in to the wonderful aroma of

Cuban food. I could always recognize the smell of arroz con pollo and potato balls. In the kitchen, we found Zerek putting the finishing touches on our plates. This man was fine, had money, and could cook. Girl code be damned, I had to have a piece of him. There was an itch that needed to be scratched and I had to start plotting soon. Zerek looked up and smiled at us.

"Where is the Cuban spot? I must go tomorrow!" I exclaimed as I sat down at the island.

"This is little Havana, Kiyana. I cooked this myself."

"Yeah, right."

Candace walked over and kissed Zerek near his mouth. He smiled as she did so. "No," she said, "he's telling the truth. He cooked this. He's an amazing chef."

"I'll be the judge of that. Candace, you've had my abuela's arroz con pollo. If it's half as good as hers, then there's some truth to your statement."

Zerek smiled at me and winked. "Then get a taste and find out."

"Oh, I will," I said, my voice dripping with honey. I took a bite of the arroz con pollo. It was amazing. I definitely had to give him something good for this. Zerek stared at me. There was an intensity in his eyes as he watched me savor every bite. He licked his lips and a few times and even winked at me. Although it was turning me on, I was shocked at how blatant he was with his flirting. I tried to avoid his gaze because I didn't want Candace noticing. She could always read my face and I didn't need the headache of having to explain anything. I looked over to see if she noticed anything, but she was too busy, checking emails on her phone. When she finally looked up from her phone screen, Zerek looked over at her and kissed her on the cheek. I saw her blush with love. Candace really had no clue to what was about to happen.

CHAPTER 7

After dinner, Zerek and Candace asked me to join them in their personal movie theatre to watch the director's cut of Captain America. As we settled into our seats, Zerek glanced at Candace and smiled. He grabbed her hand and squeezed it. "I gotta make another run to Miami on Monday. I ain't been in a minute, but my connections told me about a new investment opportunity out there that can bring in some serious money," he said excitedly.

I saw Candace's eyes light up as she turned to him. "Miami? Can I go with you?"

Zerek shook his head no. "I would love for you to come with me baby, since you haven't been home in a few years, but it's best I handle this alone. Plus, you have your launch to worry about."

Candace nodded her head in disappointment. She began to sulk in her chair. Although I'd only been up here for about two weeks, it felt like it had been years since I'd been home. I missed Miami. The sun didn't shine the same way here as it does in Miami, but I knew that if I went back home, there would be some problems. I also needed to check up on my family, though. I deep down knew that they were safe, but with Ty's crazy ass, he might have shown up and showed his ass. Zerek leaned over and kissed Candace gently on the forehead, breaking me out of my thoughts.

"I will take you anywhere you want to go. Just let me handle business," he said soothingly.

She smiled and nodded. Zerek reached over and picked up a remote. The lights dimmed and the movie started. We watched in silence, and after it was over, Zerek went upstairs to pack and I made my way to the guesthouse. I tossed and turned in my bed, sweat dripping all over my body, which was strange because I had the AC running. I got up, pulled on a thin hoodie, and stood outside.

As I stood on the steps of the guest home, I was able to see through the double doors into the kitchen. It must have been around 1 AM, but I saw Candace and Zerek leaning against the island. I watched as my best friend wrapped her legs around Zerek's hips and threw her head back in pleasure. His hips moved back and forth as he pushed Candace back and put his left hand around her neck, slightly choking her. I became excited, secretly imagining myself as Candace, feeling Zerek slide in and out of my body. He would be a perfect fit. I didn't want to get caught staring so I went back inside, hopped in my bed and went to sleep.

Later on that morning, I watched Zerek kiss Candace on the lips as she walked him to the front door. Before entering the car, he waved goodbye to her and drove off. She closed the door behind her and walked towards the stairs. Before going up the stairs, she saw me in the kitchen and walked towards me.

"So starting tonight, it's gonna be just me and you."

I smiled. "Like old times, except we're in Jersey."

Candace laughed. "So are you ready for your first day of work?"

I shrugged. "As ready as I will be."

"Are you taking an Uber or the Audi?" she asked, as she poured herself a glass of orange juice.

"I gotta get to know the area, since I'll be here for a while, so I'll drive the car. I have Waze."

"Girl, why don't you just call it a GPS, like normal people." She joked.

I playfully rolled my eyes, "Now you know we are far from normal…Especially my ass"

"Ain't that the truth." Candace laughed.

"Well good luck on your first day honey. I gotta go back to the office also. We'll catch up later." She said before walking out of the kitchen. I grabbed an apple out of the fruit basket and walked out the front door towards the car. I put the address into my phone and I was off to my new job. This was going to be the only day that I'd come in the morning, since after that they wanted to put me on the swing shift. I was to work three days a week with 12-hour shifts. Piece of cake. I could also negotiate which days, which meant I could always keep my weekends free.

The drive took roughly an hour. Traffic was horrendous. When I finally got there, I checked in and began my day. I really loved working with children. They were still loving, and still innocent, and they were optimistic despite sometimes being in terrible circumstances. I tended to stay in the pediatric divisions that didn't deal with terminal illness, though. I didn't think I could deal with watching kids die from horrible diseases. I had watched my younger sister deal with cancer when she was eight years old and although she survived, I saw the toll it took on her body. I couldn't imagine how it would have been if she died. Watching her go through that was the main reason why I became a pediatric nurse. They gave me an eight-hour day for my first day, so I was able to head home at four o'clock.

Just as I was driving up to the house, Candace was getting out of her car and heading towards the stairs. I parked in front of the house and got out of the car. She looked up as she opened the door and stepped inside.

"Hey. How was your day?"

"It was good," I answered, "I'll be starting the 12-hour shifts soon. They're breaking me in slowly."

She nodded as she closed the door behind us. "That's better than ordeal by fire."

"Tell me about it. How was your day?" I asked as we headed upstairs to the family room.

"It was good. I was just looking over the final prints. I got a surprise for you." Candace reached into her Louis Vuitton briefcase and took out a manila folder. I opened it up and my eyes widened with surprise. "Next time we have a shoot, I'll invite you so you can meet her. You just gotta stay hush about it. No telling the girls. Deal?"

I smiled. "Bet."

We sat down on the couch and turned on the TV. "Zerek stopped by my offices and we had lunch together before he left for Miami. I'm gonna miss that man."

"So since you asked questions about me and Ty," I started.

Candace narrowed her eyes at me. "In which we still aren't done with that conversation."

"How's married life?"

I watched Candace's face light up. "Well, we've had our ups and downs, as all couples do, but I really do truly love that man like no other. I know people, especially my family, thought I was stupid for marrying someone I'd only known for four months, but I can say we have really grown together."

"What kind of ups and downs did you have?"

"Nothing too bad—just the normal married mess. He does sometimes go out of town for weeks at a time, but he always makes sure to FaceTime me and to send little tokens of affection. Do I hate when he's out a lot? Yes. But they always said if you want to have a successful man, you'll have to deal with a busy one. There's pros and cons to everything."

"Sounds great," I replied.

Candace stared wistfully at the TV. "It is. Like I said, it ain't all lollipops and kittens, but we love each other so much and I'm so happy he's mine for life. The few guys I did care about actually prepared me for this man."

I felt a little pang of jealousy over my best friend's happiness. We were the same age and grew up in the same area, but our lives turned out so differently. She had her share of heart-breaks—mainly normal guys who just didn't know how to appreciate an amazing woman like her—but she finally found her king. I admit I had a thing for the bad boys and the ballers, and I knew they were no good for me, but they always gave me what I needed even at the expense of my own sanity. Yet, none of them made the effort to make me theirs. They always saw me as replaceable.

Zerek was the perfect mix. I could tell he was a good man, but he had bad boy tendencies. I was insanely attracted to him and fought the urges to come at him constantly. Being around him only made things worse. I was so happy he was out of town for a few weeks so I could get a handle on those feelings. Zerek was Candace's husband. I had to be loyal to my girl.

CHAPTER 8

While finishing my last shift at work for the week, I decided to check my emails. All had been quiet on the western front in terms of Ty. I was worried at first, since he did threaten to find me, but as I thought, it was all talk. The fact that there were no texts or calls from him just confirmed everything. He probably found a new girl to mess with that took his mind off me. I felt a little pang of sadness, but relief also because I knew I was truly free.

As I opened up my Gmail account and checked into my filter folder, I saw that Ty had sent three new emails to me, however. I checked the dates on them and they were all sent today. I didn't know whether I should open them or not.

Just as I was about to, a text message was sent to me. It was from Candace. I opened my phone and read it.

"Hey girl,

When the cat's away, the mice can play. Every day is an adventure with your bestie by your side. Let's explore the northeast together. I promise I won't only keep it in the Garden State. We're gonna take Manhattan by storm. The Big Apple ain't ready. See you after work."

Candace was right. The Big Apple ain't ready. The next week was like the good old days in Miami. In Zerek's absence, Candace took me all over Manhattan and Newark. We spent our days working and our nights at the hottest bars and dining spots in Manhattan. Our weekend consisted of shopping at Chanel and Moschino. She also treated me to a mani/pedi and a facial at Bliss Labs.

New York was everything they said and more. It was packed with hot spots and even hotter guys, and ballers with real money. Miami boys made their dough from illegal hustles, but the men here managed hedge funds and real estate developments. They weren't as fine as the South Beach boys, but they had their charm— mainly those black cards. More than a few times at the various bars we visited after work, we had drinks sent our way, and we gladly accepted them. I still was a little weary of Ty, but I decided to go against my normal M.O. and give myself some time to heal before I put myself out there in the dating world again. I might just find my Prince Charming here after all.

The medical center continued to give me eight-hour days, although they paid me for the three-twelve schedule. I had no complaints whatsoever. I just enjoyed the chance to really hang with my girl. She also made a special point to show me the different parts of New Jersey, and I realized that the area really wasn't that bad. It was less hustle and bustle than Manhattan, but it had its charm. There were also some cuties here too. Most were the blue-collar types, but I was on a mission for my happy ever after, and a construction worker was not part of the story.

Today, we decided to eat locally. Candace took me to Casa Vasca, where we dined on paella, lobster and sangria.

After taking a sip of wine, she asked me, "So now that it's been over two weeks since you've been here, what do you officially think of the northeast?"

"Actually, I like it. It's different from where we grew up, but then again there's no other place like Miami in the world. But this isn't as bad as I thought it would be, though, and there's some actual cuties here."

"Yea, the Italian boys out here are a different breed. They aren't as flashy as the South Beach boys. It's a different atmosphere. They're all about the machismo but not as in your face. They actually treat you like a lady. You should try it sometime."

"Well part of me being treated like a lady involves spending ridiculous amounts of money on me and still being solvent, so...."

"I hope you grow out of that one day."

"I hope so too," I said sarcastically. It was easy for her to say when she had a man who would and was able to give her everything she ever desired. "So how are things going for you at work?" I continued.

"We are placing ourselves in a few magazines, like Essence, Vanity Fair and Bazaar. We feel it'll expose us to a different audience and expand our brand. We are also looking at creating a capsule collection with a few actresses for this ensemble movie they're working on."

"That sounds so exciting. I sometimes wish that I went the route that you and Anais went. It's so glam."

"It's cool, but what you do for work is what really makes a difference. Plus, you have to be a special kind of person to do what you do. You need brains and compassion, and not many people have that combination. We all have our place in the world."

I had to agree with her on that. The waiter came over and poured us another glass of sangria. Although Candace tried to appease me, I couldn't shake the nagging feeling that she was telling me to settle for what I could get. I really hated when people told me that. If I saw that others could have it all, why couldn't I have the same thing? Over the past few days, my feelings for Zerek had begun to fade, but they flared right back up again. Candace took out her wallet and paid for our dinner. She might just end up paying for more than that.

We came home and went straight to bed. I sat in the guesthouse, trying to get over this petty feeling I was having toward my best friend.

I honestly had to figure out where it came from. Why was I so angry with her? She was happy and successful, which were things I honestly wanted for all of my girls, but sometimes things she would say and do would get under my skin. I looked at my surroundings and began to feel guilty. Candace opened her home to me in my time of need. I shouldn't be so ungrateful for the kindness she showed me. She wasn't perfect, but she was damn near close to it.

I decided to take a long shower to see if I could wash away those feelings. I walked into the bathroom, undressed, tied my hair up and stepped into the hot shower. The hot, steamy water felt wonderful against my skin. I took my bath lily and started lathering up. As I soaped up my body, my mind began to wander. I began to imagine what Zerek's hands would feel like caressing my body. The tiny droplets of water became his kisses. I had to get these thoughts out of my head. I shook my head to clear my mind, then hurriedly finished bathing and turned off the faucet. I lotioned myself up with my Caudalie lotion and put on my pajamas.

I woke up late the next day and made my way to the kitchen. Today was my day off, but I knew Candace would be at work. I thought I would veg out today and watch another movie in their theatre. As I approached the kitchen, I was pleasantly surprised to see Zerek there, cooking. I only had a sleep hoodie on over my pajamas, which were only a pair of sleep shorts and a camisole. I felt my nipples slightly harden as I watched him. This was going to be tough. I made a lot of noise as I walked through the sliding door and sat at the island. He turned around, gave me a once-over and then smiled.

"Well, hello there," he said flirtatiously.

I tried to keep my voice calm. "So you're back early? I thought you weren't going to be home for at least another week. I know I would've made it last as long as possible. Ain't no place like Miami."

Zerek nodded. "That's true, but I finished the deal early and I missed my woman, so I had to come back home. I was going to surprise her at work later on."

"That is so sweet of you. You two are definitely my marriage goals. You're a good man," I responded.

"She brings it out of me," Zerek said and smiled as he turned his back on me. I watched as he sautéed some chicken and veggies in the pan, before he turned back to me.

"So where did you learn how to cook?"

"Prison!" Zerek exclaimed. My eyes widened and he started laughing hysterically.

"I'm playing with you, man. You think Candace would really mess with a jail nigga?" He continued, "It's just something I like to do. It's kind of an escape from the daily shit I deal with. It's one of my many talents."

I raised my eyebrow. Licking my lips slightly, I smiled seductively at him. "So what else are you good at?"

Zerek leaned over the island and lowered his eyes at me. "What do you want to know exactly?"

I leaned over also. "Whatever you feel comfortable with telling me?"

"Well, just as good as I can cook, I can also eat."

I bit my lower lip and slightly shook in response. He watched my reaction and smiled slightly.

"I'm also very good at risk-taking, too. Every risk I took in life, whether if it was business or personal, I've always came out on top. Candace was a major risk to me. Marrying a chick I'd only known for only four months was a big one, but it definitely paid off. Meeting her has exposed me to quite a bit of good fortune." He winked at me as he said this. He turned around again and walked over to the stove, then poured some rice into the steamer and turned it on.

"Would you like to help me cook? I still need some help." He asked me.

I walked over to the stove and stood next to him. "So what are you cooking?"

"One of Candace's favorites. Chicken stir fry with jasmine rice."

"So what do you need my help with?" I asked.

He turned to me and licked his lips again. "Taste testing," he said seductively. He picked up a spoon and dipped it on the saucepan. I stepped closer to him as he removed the spoon from the pan. He smelled so good. Between the scent of his cologne and the close proximity to his body, my hips began to respond. If he made any move, I knew I would be his. I knew I should have moved away from him, but sometimes I liked playing with fire. Zerek blew on the spoon to cool off the sauce and ran it gently across my lips. I licked the sauce off my lips and the spoon. He took a deep, ragged breath as he watched me.

"It's delicious," I said.

He smiled again, while still staring at my lips. "It's homemade."

"A man of many talents."

"Many. So are you thirsty?"

"You have no idea," I said absentmindedly and smiled. Zerek laughed.

"Girl, you ain't never lied," he said. I immediately felt embarrassed and I knew it showed on my face. Oh My God! Was it that obvious? I'd been called many things, but thirsty was not one of them. I always had to push them off me. I was so used to men coming on to me strong that I didn't know how to react when they were subtle. I had to reclaim my cool.

He walked over to the built-in wine cooler and took out a bottle and two glasses, then popped the cork. After he poured, he handed a glass to me and I took a sip. It was a merlot. Very sweet, very fruity, and my kind of drink.

"I have more from where that came from," he said to me. "So drink up."

"So what else are we cooking?" I asked.

"Well, we have the stir fry, rice and sauce. Do you know how to make crème brulee?"

"I know how to eat it," I said laughing.

"I'm sure you do. It's easy. I already prepared the actual dessert. All we need to do is just caramelize the sugar and that's it."

"I think I can do that," I responded after taking another sip.

"I know you can," He said, winking again. Zerek gulped down the rest of his wine and refilled his glass, then mine. Heading to the refrigerator, he reached in and pulled out three crème brulee bowls, then went to the cabinet for some sugar. Setting the bowls on the island in front of me, he sprinkled sugar on top of each one.

"What kind of crème brulee is this?" I asked. It had a slightly pink tone to it.

"It's raspberry crème brulee. I put Candace up on game about this one. It's pretty good. You'll like it."

He then reached into a drawer and pulled out a lighter. Walking up and standing behind me, he took my arms and handed me the lighter. He pressed his body against mine. I could really smell his cologne and felt his thick bulge, which began to get hard as he pressed it against my butt. My body began to melt against his.

"Now, flick on the flame and gently move the lighter from side to side in a downward motion. This makes the sugar harden." As he said that, he rubbed his hardening dick against my body. I shivered. He guided my arms as I flicked on the lighter. I moved my arms back and forth over the bowls and watched as the sugar turned a light brown and became a thick shell over the crème brulee.

"Like that?"

Zerek leaned over and whispered in my ear. "Yeah, like that." I pushed my body against his. His left hand gently caressed my naked thigh.

When we finished, I turned around and stared at him.

"All finished," he said. He smiled and walked over to the other side of the island. In one big gulp, he finished his glass of merlot. He then took the half-filled bottle and placed it back in the wine cooler. I just stood there, hoping that he couldn't see the wetness that was starting to form between my thighs. I had to compose myself. I leaned over and finished my last few sips of the wine, then walked over to the cabinets and took out three plates and three glasses. I placed them on the island in front of the three stools. Zerek walked over to the stove and turned off the food, before looking at his watch.

"Candace should be coming home in about an hour. Everything is almost ready." He announced. He washed his hands and dried them off on the table, then finished setting the places.

Zerek walked over to the entrance to the kitchen and turned to me, motioning for me to follow him. "Hey Kiyana, come with me right quick. I have something to show you."

I went to follow him. "Where are we going?"

He gave me another onceover and winked. "Just follow me, please."

I nodded my head and shrugged my shoulders. "Lead the way."

We walked out of the kitchen and toward the stairs.

EPILOGUE

We walked past the family room to their bedroom. I tried to hold my composure. I was going into the bedroom with my best friend's gorgeous husband, whom I happened to be attracted to. I shouldn't have followed him into his room. I had to do something. Zerek walked in and I stood at the door.

"I can wait outside," I said. Zerek turned to me and laughed, shaking his head. He walked back towards me.

"What are you so afraid of?" he teased.

"I ain't scared of nothing."

"I just wanted to show you a few things. Since you're rooming with us, you should also know a few things about me too. So come on. Don't be a punk."

I laughed and shook my head. "Fine!" I said and walked into the bedroom. Just as I expected, their bedroom was fucking gorgeous! It fit the motif of the rest of the house. There was a white Cali King bed adorned with a beautiful turquoise and gold bed linens, and I had to force the thought of him pinning me against the bed and ripping my clothes off out of my head. The rest of the room was decorated with a white, art deco style dresser and nightstands. A teal leather armchair and ottoman stood in the corner next to a white table that held a couple of sketchbooks, some pencils and a vase of white calla lilies. Three Michael Massenburg paintings finished off the décor of the room.

"I always wondered why Candace decorated every single room with white, turquoise and yellow," I said.

Zerek laughed. "She said she wanted something that reminded her of Miami. White sand beaches, golden yellow sun and turquoise seas."

I nodded. "That definitely sounds like my girl. So what'd you want to show me?"

Zerek walked over to the table and picked

up one of the sketchbooks, bringing it over to me as he flipped through the pages. "These are some designs for some of the buildings I want to develop."

"So that's what you do."

"Well, it's some of what I do. I own several businesses."

"So why did you guys move from Miami?"

"I was never in Miami to begin with. I was always based out here. I met Candace while out with some of my business associates. I looked at her and I swear a voice said to me, that's her. I was struck by her beauty and how she carried herself."

I felt a small pang of jealousy as I watched his face soften at the thought of her. I never saw a man look at me that way. They always looked at me with lust. Even Ty, who I had spent two years with, never looked at me that way.

"She initially didn't want to leave everything she knew, but I had to make the decision worth her while, so I gave her free reign on the kind of house and let her decorate any way she wished. The only room that is truly mine is the study. That's why it looks so different from the rest of the house."

"Makes sense," I replied.

"I would hope so."

I flipped through the pages thoroughly impressed with the designs. "Is there anything that you can't do?" I continued.

Zerek grinned. "Nothing. I gotta get comfortable." He then walked over to the dresser and took out a pair of sweats and a wife beater. He began to undress in front of me. I tried my best not to pay attention, but I felt my body begin to react

"Um, Zerek. I'll just wait outside for you." I put the book down on the table and began to walk out of the room. Just before I was able to reach the door, I felt him grab me by the arm and turn me around to face him. And there he stood. Tall, brown, and muscled. He was wearing nothing but his boxers, which only accentuated his impressive bulge. He pulled me closer to him. I was nervous. Nervous about Candace coming home and seeing this. Nervous that we would be caught, and nervous that ultimately I wouldn't care.

I looked up at him, trying to compose my face. I absentmindedly bit my lip. I didn't know how much longer I could take it, or how much longer I could hold it off. The longer I stared at him, the less resolve I had in succumbing to my attraction to him. I was definitely in trouble.

~

Find out what happens next in Taking What's Hers Book 2! Available Now!

To find out when Mia Black has new books available, **follow Mia Black on Instagram: @authormiablack**

TAKING WHAT'S HERS 2

Kiyana has done the unthinkable. Now regretting the one move that will ultimately ruin her friendship, Kiyana has to keep her dirty little secret like her life depends on it. She vows to leave Zerek alone, but it's easier said than done.

Find out what happens in part two of Taking What's Hers!

To find out when Mia Black has new books available, **follow Mia Black on Instagram: @authormiablack**

CPSIA information can be obtained
at www.ICGtesting.com
Printed in the USA
LVHW081755200820
663728LV00017B/1448